© 1993 Geddes & Grosset Ltd
Published by Geddes & Grosset Ltd,
New Lanark, Scotland.

ISBN 1 85534 590 0

Printed and bound in Italy.

The Wily Fox and the Little Red Hen

Retold by Judy Hamilton
Illustrated by R. James Binnie

Tarantula Books

Once upon a time in a little house in the woods, there lived a little red hen. The woods were a dangerous place for a little bird like this, but she loved her little house and was usually very careful and sensible as she went about her chores.

There lived in the same woods a wily old fox. He wanted badly to catch the little red hen, for she would make a tasty dinner for him.

He had chosen the pot he would use to cook her in, and he watched her every day, waiting for a chance to catch her.

But the little red hen knew about the fox and his tricks, and was always careful to avoid being caught.

However, we all make mistakes, and one day the little red hen left her house and forgot to lock the door behind her. She strutted out into the woods to look for sticks for her fire. As the hen pecked busily about among the trees, building a pile of sticks, the fox noticed the open door of her house, and saw his chance to catch her at last.

He waited until she was out of sight and then slipped up the steps and inside the front door. He hid behind a cupboard and waited for the little red hen. As he waited, he thought about the recipe he would use when cooking her for his dinner.

After a while, the hen returned home and struggled up the steps with her big bundle of sticks. She put the sticks down on the top step and put her key in the front door, but it opened before she turned the key, and she realised that she had left it unlocked.

"How careless of me!" the little red hen thought. "Anybody could have gone into my house while I was out!"

And she was right. As she stepped inside, the wily fox pounced at her.

Luckily, the little red hen was just too quick for him. She flapped and fluttered up to a perch high in the rafters, out of the fox's reach.

"Ha-ha, Mr Fox!" she cackled merrily from her perch. "You'll never get me up here! It looks like you've missed another chance to catch me. Why don't you go away and dig up some slugs for your supper instead?"

The wily fox was angry and frustrated, but he was determined not to give up as easily as that.

He lay down on the floor and began to think.

Never one to be idle, the little red hen sat on her perch preening her petticoats as she waited for the fox to leave.

But a long time passed and still the fox did not leave.

The little red hen looked down from her high perch and looked at the wily fox lying on the floor.

"Aren't you getting bored yet, Mr Fox?" she asked him cheekily.

"As a matter of fact, I am," replied the fox, getting to his feet. There was a gleam in his eye. "I think I'll play a little game."

With that, the fox began to turn slowly round and round, trying to catch his tail in his mouth.

The little red hen watched him from above as he continued to chase his tail. He began to speed up, running round and round in a circle on the floor below the little red hen's perch.

The little red hen could not understand why the fox was doing this, but nevertheless she watched him as he spun round faster and faster. Then she began to feel a little peculiar.

"Mr Fox," she said rather weakly, "please stop, I'm feeling dizzy!"

But the wily fox continued to whirl round faster than ever chasing his tail, and the faster he went, the dizzier the poor little hen became.

She began to sway backwards and forwards on her perch.

Faster and faster went the fox, until finally the little red hen became so dizzy that she fainted and fell down off her perch and landed on the floor beside the fox with a 'thump!'

Quick as a flash, the fox stopped chasing his tail and grabbed a sack that was hanging on the back of the door. Before the poor little red hen had a chance to recover, that wily fox bundled her up, higgledy piggledy, into the sack and tied the top with string.

"Chicken for dinner—how perfectly delicious!" said the fox to himself, his mouth beginning to water in anticipation. "You weren't such a clever little red hen after all!" he told the bundle in the sack.

Then the fox picked up the sack, slung it over his shoulder, and set off for home.

The little red hen, who was beginning to recover, wriggled and struggled to get out of the sack, but in vain.

The wily fox marched through the woods at a good pace, carrying his wriggling dinner. The hen was heavy and awkward to carry, but the fox didn't mind because he could only think of how tasty she would be. After a while, the hen stopped struggling and lay quietly.

"The hen must have gone to sleep," thought the fox. "Sure enough, it must be hot in that sack." He continued on his way for a few moments and then he stopped.

"It's hot out here as well," he thought, "and this hen is heavy. I think I'll rest for a while."

He put down his sack and lay down under a tree to rest. In two minutes, the fox was fast asleep.

Inside the sack, the hen, however, was not asleep. Hearing the snores of the fox, she acted quickly. There was a tiny hole in the bottom of the sack and the hen set to work pecking at the edges of the hole to make it bigger. It did not take long to make it just big enough for her to squeeze out. Once she was free, she scuttled over to a stream close to where the fox was sleeping. Pushing and shoving with all her might, she rolled three great big stones, one by one, out of the stream and over to where the sack lay. One by one, she rolled them into the sack. It was hard work, and she had to be quiet so as not to wake the fox.

At last, all the stones were in the sack.

There was just one more thing to do. Pecking off a bit of the string that fastened the top of the sack, the hen quickly used it to tie up the hole which she had made in the bottom when she had crawled out. The little red hen smiled to herself. Everything was ready. She hid behind a bush and waited for the fox to wake up.

After a few minutes the fox yawned, stretched, stood up, swung the sackful of stones over his shoulder and set off once again towards his house. The little red hen followed at a safe distance, careful not to be spotted by the fox.

"Phew! This hen seems to be getting heavier and heavier!" grunted the fox as he lugged the sack of stones towards his front door, "I will be glad when I can get her out of this bag and into the stockpot."

Safely hidden some way behind the fox, the little red hen tried not to laugh out loud. The wily fox was in for a shock! Puffing and panting, the fox heaved the sack inside his house and put it down.

From outside the window the hen peeked in and saw the fox put a big pot of water on the fire to boil.

"All that hard work has given me an appetite!" said the fox as he began to prepare some vegetables.

The hen watched while the fox chopped and sliced and peeled, waiting for the water to boil.

When the water was boiling, the fox stopped what he was doing and picked up the sack. The hen hid her eyes. She didn't want to see what happened next.

The fox tipped the sack up over the pot. 'SPLASH! SPLASH! SPLASH!'

The three great big stones fell in the water one by one. Boiling water splashed over everything, including the fox. He was killed in an instant.

The little red hen turned away and scuttled off home. She had shown that she was cleverer than the wily fox. Life would be much safer in the woods from now on.